This edition first published 1999
by Hodder Children's Books
A division of Hodder Headline plc
338 Euston Road
London NW1 3BH

A catalogue record for this book is available from
the British Library

ISBN 0 340 71667 3

Printed and bound in Great Britain

Postman Pat™
and the
Spring Fair

John Cunliffe
Illustrated by Stuart Trotter

from the original television
designs by **Ivor Wood**

h
Hodder
Children's
Books

a division of Hodder Headline plc

Chapter One
The spider

It was springtime in Greendale.
There were lambs in the fields,
daffodils in all the gardens . . .

and a big spider under
Julian's bed.
"A spider!" shouted Pat.
"Help! I'm off!"
"It won't hurt you," said
Julian. "It's dead."

"It's all dried up," said Sara.
"It must have been there a
long time," said Pat.
"And that means . . ." said
Sara . . .

"I know," said Julian. "It's a long time . . ."
" . . . since you cleaned under that bed," said Sara.

Julian went to get the vacuum cleaner. He poked the long sucker-tube at the spider.

Its legs waved in the breeze
for a moment, and Pat thought
it had come back to life. Then
it went *whoosh*, sucked away
with a pile of fluff.

"There you are!" said Julian.
"Don't stop," said Sara.
"It's gone," said Julian.
"There was only one,"
said Pat.

"What a pair of gobbins,"
said Sara. "There's enough
fluff under that bed to fill a
cushion."
Julian fitted the sweeper tool
to the vacuum cleaner, and
pushed it under the bed.

He liked vacuuming. He loved
the growl of the motor, and the
way it sucked the dust up.

"How's that?" said Julian.
"Fine," said Sara. "Tell you
what. Just keep going."
"Round the edges first. Under
that chair. Under
your desk.

Don't forget the window-ledges. Then, when you've finished your room, there's our room, the stairs, the sitting-room . . ."
"Oh no!" said Julian.
"Oh yes," said Sara.

Chapter Two

We can't miss the football

"We can't miss the football,"
said Pat.
"Haven't you two noticed?"
said Sara.

"What?" said Pat and Julian
together.
"Well, look out of that window.
What can you see?"

"It's a nice day for a game
of football," said Julian.
"A great day for a game of
football," said Pat.
"A grand day for spring-
cleaning," said Sara.

Pat and Julian looked so sad!

"All right," said Sara. "Go
to the football. But, think on,
it's half-term next week.
Spring-cleaning starts on
Monday, and no later."

"Oh, heck!" said Pat. "I know
what that means."
"So do I," said Julian.
"A big clear-out, for one thing,"
said Sara, "and a big tidy-up."

"We know!" said Julian.
"We know!" said Pat. "Mind
you, I'll have a lot of letters
to tidy-up, first."

Chapter Three
A big pile of toys!

It was a grand game of
football. Pencaster won
3-0 against Carlisle. It was
their first big win for years.

"That's because they've put
Ted Glen in goal," said Pat.
"He's the best goalie they've
ever had."

Pat went off with the post on Monday morning. Julian and Sara started the clearing out and tidying up. Jess found some mice in the cupboard under the stairs, and chased them out into the garden.

"There's more rubbish in
this house than there is on
Pencaster tip!" said Sara.
Julian made a big pile of all
his toys and games in the
middle of the floor.

17

"I'm not putting all this on the tip!" he said.

"Now, then," said Sara, "we'll not put them all on the tip. Sort them out into three lots.

One: everything that's broken
and useless. They're for the tip.
Two: things you don't want to
play with again. They can go
to a jumble sale. And . . .
three: things you want to keep.
They can be put away, nice
and tidy."
"Right!" said
Julian, setting
to work.

Chapter Four

Getting sorted

Sara did the same thing all
over the house. When Pat
came home, she set him on as
well.

There were soon little piles
of things everywhere.
They had labels on them . . .

When Julian looked at his
'KEEP' pile, it felt like
Christmas all over again.

There were so many things
that had been lost at the back
of the cupboard. He couldn't
wait to play with them again.

The other two piles were quite
big enough. They made space
for the things he wanted to
keep.

Sara and Pat found all sorts
of things they had forgotten
about. Pat collected six teapots
in the kitchen.

"Well, that one can go," said
Sara, pointing at a really weird
teapot. "I never did like it."

Chapter Five

The Spring Fair

The next day, Pat saw a
poster outside the church.
'GREENDALE CHURCH
SPRING FAIR' it said.

When Pat gave the Reverend
Timms his post, he said,
"I hope you can bring
something for the Spring
Fair, Pat?"

"Oh, don't worry about that,"
said Pat. "We'll fill every stall.
You should just see our house!

I don't know how there's room
for us to get in it."

There were ten boxes of things for the Spring Fair. Alf came with his tractor, and took them all to the Church Hall one windy Thursday afternoon.

The dustbin-men took away
five bags of rubbish the same
day.

"That's better," said Sara.
"We've got room to turn
around, now."

All over Greendale, folks were getting things ready for the Spring Fair, polishing things up to look like new. Dorothy Thompson and Miss Hubbard were busy making cakes and biscuits for the cake stall.

Granny Dryden was knitting
at top speed.

Jess found a quiet
place in a barn,
with the bats
and the owls,
and stayed
there until
it was
all over.

Julian saved his pocket money
up. There were always some
good bargains at the Spring
Fair. You could get computer
games for fifty pence sometimes.

Chapter Six
A special present!

The day of the fair came at last. There was a line of people outside the village hall, waiting for the Reverend Timms to unlock the door.

What a rush there was!
Everybody wanted to be
first at Dorothy Thompson's
cake stall.

Then they flocked around
the pots and pans,

the toys and games,
the second-hand books . . .

. . . the hats and dresses. All
the things the people of
Greendale had turned out of
drawers and cupboards for the
Spring Fair.

They all bought something to
take home with them, and
there was a good collection
of money for the church. It
was a great Spring Fair.

Julian spent all his pocket
money. He found three
computer games he had never
seen before, and he bought a
present for Pat and Sara.

It was a teapot. A very
curious teapot. He thought
he might have seen one like it,
somewhere, long ago. He felt
sure they would love it.

They collected teapots, so they
would be certain to like this
one, even though it was a bit
strange.

He had it wrapped up, so
that it would be a surprise.

"What have you bought?"
said Sara.
"Wait and see," said Julian.

Chapter Seven

A big surprise

When they unwrapped the
teapot on the kitchen table,
they both said, "Oh!"

Then Sara said, "Oh . . . dear!"
And Pat said, "Well, I never!"
And Julian said, "What's up?"

"It's this teapot," said Sara.
"We sent it to the sale,"
said Pat.
"Oh," said Julian. "I thought
you'd like it, to add to your
collection."

"He won't have seen it before,"
said Pat, "because . . ."
"Never mind," said Sara.
"Let's have a nice cup of tea
out of it."

Pat poured tea for everyone.
"I'd forgotten it dribbled," said
Sara, as tea splattered all over
the tablecloth. Never mind. It
was a very kind thought.
Thank you, Julian."

"Yes . . ." said Pat. "Nice tea, anyway."
"I wonder if we'll ever get rid of this blessed pot?" said Sara.

Chapter Eight
Ted saves the day

Ted Glen called in on Tuesday
afternoon.
"Have a cup of tea," said Pat.

"Thanks," said Ted. "My,
that's a grand teapot. I've
been looking for one like that
for years, for my antique shop.
You can't get them these days,
you just can't get them."

"It is unusual," said Pat.
"Where did you get it?"
asked Ted.

"Julian bought it at the
Spring Fair," said Sara,
"as a surprise."
"It was more of a surprise
than he thought," said Pat.

"I was sorry to miss that fair," said Ted. "Now then, if you ever want to sell that pot, I'd offer a good price."

"I don't think they really want it," said Julian. "You see, it's one they'd sent to the fair, but I didn't know it was ours!"

Chapter Nine

It's a deal!

"Oh, bless me," said Ted,
laughing. "What a mix-up!"

" . . . tell you what. If you sold it to me, you could buy them something else for a real surprise, next time you go to Pencaster."

"That's a good idea," said
Julian.
"Now, then," said Ted, "would
you take twenty pounds for it?"
"Yes!" said Julian. "I certainly
would."

"I think it's a fair price,"
said Ted.
"It's a deal," said Julian.
Ted counted the money
into his hand.

That night, there was another
spider under Julian's bed.
This one was very much alive.

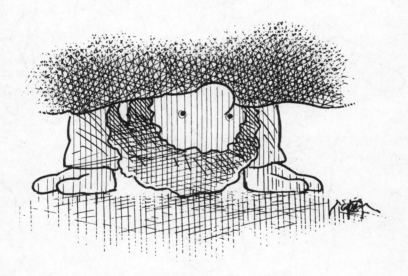

"Don't tell Mum," said Pat.
"It can wait for next year's
spring-cleaning."

This Book Belongs To

. . . .

STR		ALC	
SHI		ALM	
SHM		SDL	2/01
KIN		HEN	
WEL		SOU	
HRB		SOM